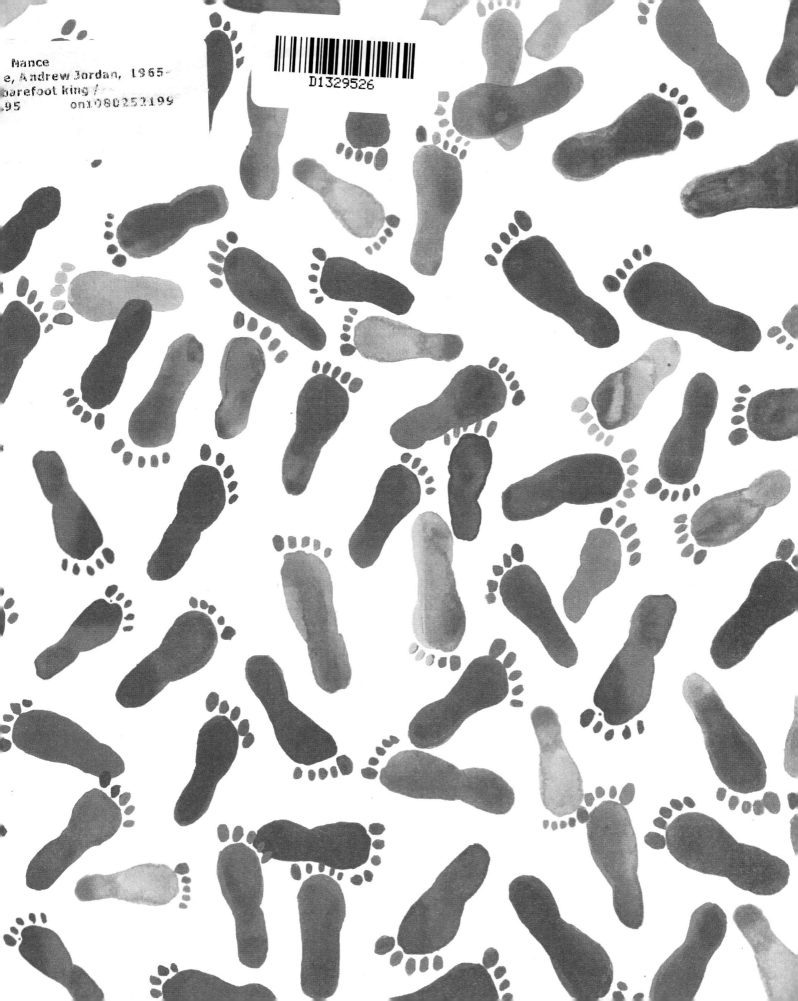

Bala Kids
An imprint of Shambhala Publications, Inc.
4720 Walnut Street
Boulder, Colorado 80301
www.shambhala.com

9 8 7 6 5 4 3 2 1

First Edition
Printed in China

♾ This edition is printed on acid-free paper that meets the American National Standards Institute Z39.48 Standard.
♻ Shambhala makes every effort to print on recycled paper. For more information please visit www.shambhala.com.

Bala Kids is distributed worldwide by Penguin Random House, Inc., and its subsidiaries.

Designed by Kara Plikaitis

Library of Congress Cataloging-in-Publication Data
Names: Nance, Andrew, author. | Holden, Olivia, illustrator.
Title: The barefoot king / Andrew Jordan Nance; Illustrated by Olivia Holden.
Description: Boulder, Colorado: Bala Kids, 2020. | Summary: Young King Creet orders that the land be covered in leather so he will never again stub his bare toe, but when that proves unwise a minister proposes a better solution.
Identifiers: LCCN 2018059738 | ISBN 9781611807486 (hardcover: alk. paper)
Subjects: | CYAC: Stories in rhyme. | Kings, queens, rulers, etc.—Fiction. | Mindfulness—Fiction. | Shoes—Fiction.
Classification: LCC PZ8.3.N274 Bar 2020 | DDC [E]—dc23
LC record available at https://lccn.loc.gov/2018059738

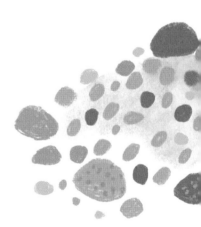

written by

Andrew Jordan Nance

illustrated by

Olivia Holden

The Barefoot King

bala kids

Long ago there was a young king named Creet.

In his land, people walked with bare feet.

King Creet was smart but had a wandering mind.

He was always tripping on things he would find.

One day he left the palace to take a walk alone.
Distracted by birds, he stubbed his toe on a stone.

The king yelled, "Ow!" and kicked the rock.
He hopped home in pain and in shock.

That night he tossed, tumbled, and turned;
the image of that rock returned and returned.

In the morning he woke with a plan and let out a cry.

He called to his ministers, "I have an idea to try!"

The ministers listened to the king's every word.

They couldn't believe the idea that they'd heard.

"I stubbed my foot while out on a walk.
   This must never happen again!" He continued to talk.

"I order you to cover this great land with leather.
   Nobody's feet shall get hurt. We'll be safe forever!"

His ministers scratched their
heads and traded baffled shrugs,

then went in search of leather
coats, curtains, and rugs.

His people sewed the leather together
one scrap at a time.

For months they stitched patches with
needles and twine.

Then they rolled out the leather all across the land:
on fields, up cliffs, down hills, over sand.

The ministers oversaw the covering of each street,
hoping this solution would calm down King Creet.

When the leather was finally laid all about,
the king felt better, until he heard people shout.

All of the kingdom came to yell and complain:
their fields could no longer catch any rain.

The plants could no longer get water to grow.
There was not one flower at the flower show.

The leather on the streets was terribly hot
and slippery when wet, believe it or not.

Young King Creet knew he had to
make things right.

He woke his ministers in the middle
of the night.

He pleaded with them to find a new resolution.

One of his wisest ministers had a solution.

She calmly said, "It is unwise to
cover this land with leather.

We can no more control the earth
than we can the weather.

"You are young, my king, but since
the beginning of time,

people have worked to train their
wandering minds."

"Instead of trying to fix what makes you squirm,

train your mind to be more aware, calm, and firm.

"With practice you will soon
notice the stones in your path.

You may still trip, but instead
of getting angry, you'll laugh."

"Life's challenges are not going to go away,
  but we can learn to be more skillful every day."

"Instead of covering each mountain and street,
let's simply put the leather right on our feet!"

The young king gasped.
The ministers became very afraid.

"A brilliant idea!" he exclaimed.
And that's how shoes were made.

Author's Note

Where would I possibly find enough leather
with which to cover the surface of the earth?
But [wearing] leather just on the soles of my shoes
is equivalent to covering the earth with it.

—Shantideva

I was inspired to write *The Barefoot King* by the teachings of an Indian scholar named Shantideva, who wrote a book over a thousand years ago called *A Guide to the Bodhisattva's Way of Life*. In it, he reminds us how our mind can protect us from the harms of the world. He compares the mind to shoes, which also protect us from harm. I wondered what it would be like if someone actually covered the land with leather and how silly that would be, and how many other problems it would create.

While this story just imagines how shoes might have come to be, historically the first-known shoes were worn in Mesopotamia, between 1600 and 1200 B.C.E. They were soft shoes made of leather similar to a moccasin and were worn by the mountain people who lived on the border of what is now Iran.

Thinking about how shoes protect our feet, we can consider how our mind can protect us from harm too. We can all practice paying more attention so that when something is difficult, we can notice it and move around it, or skillfully navigate our challenges instead of tripping over them. We can't make the whole world smooth and easy with no bumps, but we *can* learn to handle the bumps with conscious breaths and mindful steps. I hope you liked reading *The Barefoot King*, sparked by the wisdom of so long ago.

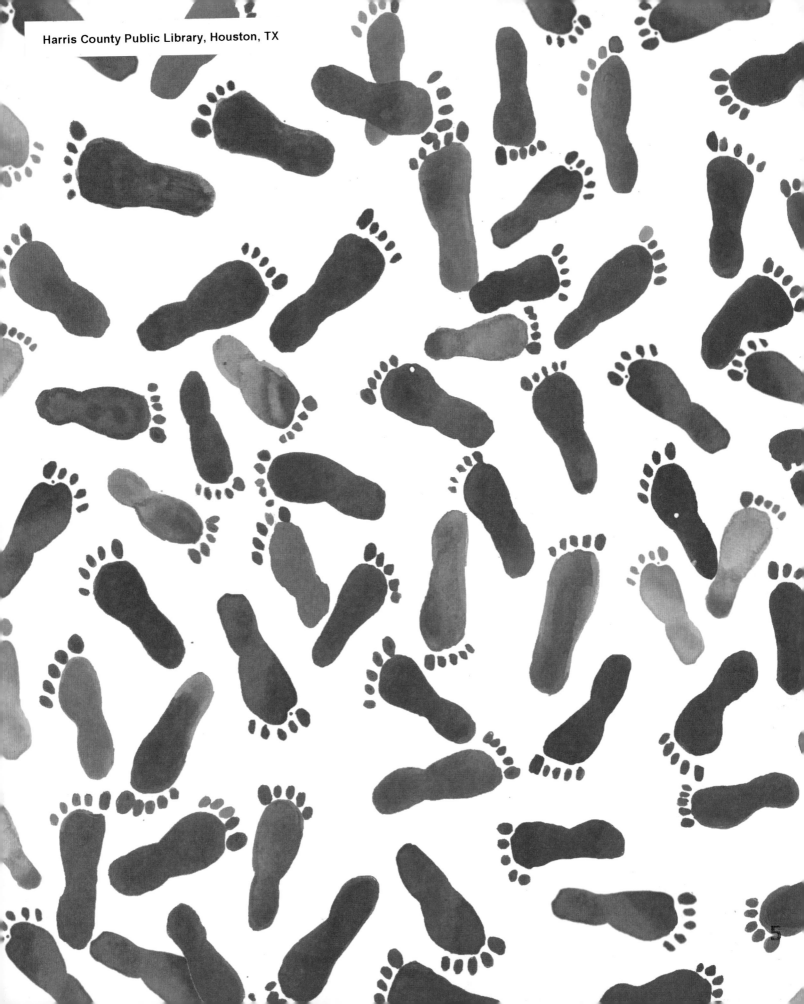

5